City in Space

Written by Sharon Wohl
Illustrated by Adam Byrne

A Better Way of Learning
Creator of The Phonics Game™

Printed in the U.S.A.

A Better Way of Learning • *www.phonicsgame.com*

We must make a city in space,
because we need a base on the moon.
We will send a crew to the moon.

Britt, Blake, Jen and Greg will be the crew
in the spacecraft.
They get into the spacesuits.

The launch time is near.
The crew stops and hopes that the trip will be safe.

It's time to go.
Close the hatch.
Strap in.

It's the countdown. Ten, nine...
Wait, the ship can't go.
They must change the day of the launch.

Now the spacecraft can take off.
10, 9, 8, 7, 6, 5, 4, 3, 2, 1...Blast off!

Greg, Jen, Britt and Blake race to the moon.
They see the globe on the screen.

They see the moon in space.

The crew unstraps
and floats in the spaceship.
It feels strange.

The moon is close.
The crew lands the spacecraft.

On the moon, it is hot and they can't breathe.
It is 260° F!
The spacesuits protect them.
The crew explores.
It seems odd with no air,
no clouds, no wind and no rain.

It takes a year to make the moon base.
Each day the spaceships land
and drop off things the crew needs.

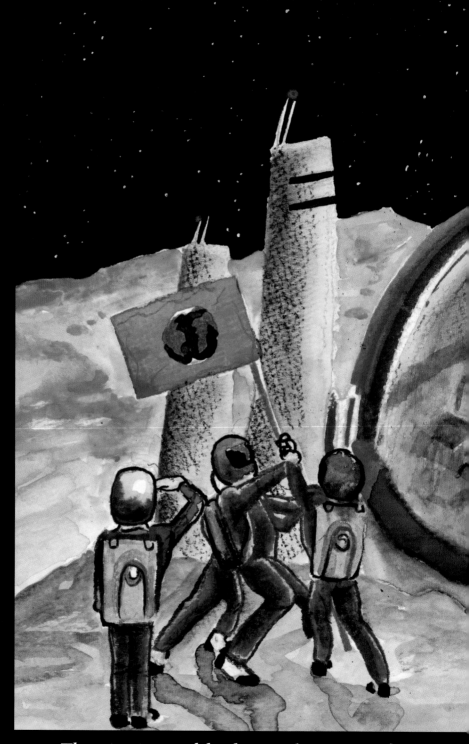

The city is not like home, but it is a fine city.

Jen, Blake, Greg and Britt lift up the flag.

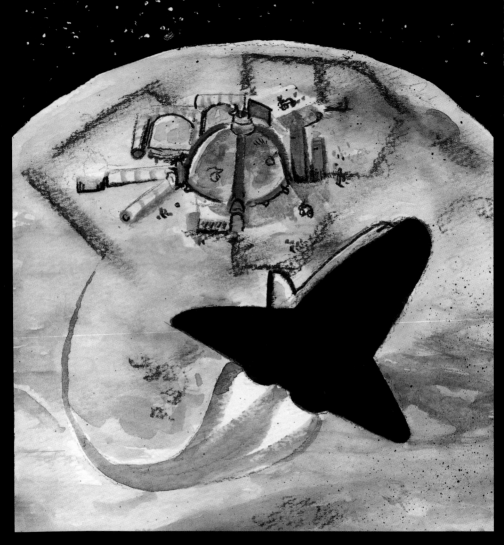

The crew will leave.
They can be proud of the job they did.
They made a new city in space!